CANARIES
AND
CRIMINALS

◎ ◎ ◎

CANARIES
AND
CRIMINALS

Kelly Easton

CANDLEWICK PRESS
CAMBRIDGE, MASSACHUSETTS

Copyright © 2003 by Kelly Easton

First edition 2003

Library of Congress Cataloging-in-Publication Data

Easton, Kelly.
Canaries and criminals / Kelly Easton. —1st ed.
p.   cm.
Summary: Aaron is pursued by ex-convicts searching for a valuable turtle
left at the pet store belonging to his parents.
ISBN 0-7636-1928-0
[1. Pet shops — Fiction. 2. Robbers and outlaws — Fiction.] I. Title.
PZ7.E13155 Can 2003
[Fic] — dc21   2002073894

2 4 6 8 10 9 7 5 3 1

Printed in the United States of America

This book was typeset in Goudy.

Candlewick Press
2067 Massachusetts Avenue
Cambridge, Massachusetts 02140

visit us at www.candlewick.com

For Isaac

⊙ ⊙ ⊙

ACKNOWLEDGMENTS

Many thanks to my husband, Arthur Jay Spivack,
to my daughter, Isabelle, and to Randi, Gordon, Michael,
Robert, and Sheli Easton, as well as to Joanne Baines
for their love and support. Thanks also to this book's superb
editor, Deborah Wayshak, to Liz Bicknell,
to the staff of Candlewick Press,
and to Jane Dystel.

chapter 1

◎ ◎ ◎ Ms. Guranga, my favorite librarian, walked toward me. With her white, fluffy hair, she reminds me of a cockatiel. She tapped the face of her watch with her claw. My half-hour was up and she was about to kick me off the computer; I could tell. I was getting better on the Internet, feeling less like some kindergartner on the first day of school. Under references for the Birdman of Alcatraz, there were seventeen sites. I'd been through six of them, but they pretty much had the same story: the Birdman's troubled relationship with his father, his closeness with his mother, his stays at various prisons — but nothing much about his theories on birds.

Guranga puffed up her feathers and started to land, but I got lucky; some old lady researching Buddhism cornered her.

"If you're Buddhist," I heard the lady say, "you get to be recycled."

"You mean, *reincarnated*," Guranga corrected.

"Same thing. An endless cycle of rebirth —"

"And death," Guranga added, throwing cold water on the old lady's cheerful hopes.

"Say you and your husband like each other in this life. Then, in your next life, you might be reborn as his next-door neighbor. Or maybe you don't like him; he's a stinker. Then *he's* reborn as your dog. You might throw him out in the yard, say, and not feed him. You might walk by and kick him."

"Oh, I wouldn't treat a dog that way."

"Even if he was your rotten, stinking husband?"

"But how could you be sure?" Guranga asked with a great deal of sincerity.

I turned my attention back to the computer. The Birdman's real name was Robert Stroud, and he lived his whole adult life in prison, seventeen years of it on Alcatraz, an island in San Francisco Bay.

"Why are you interested in some murderous maniac?"

into our shop are entering our house (which isn't far from the truth, now that we live upstairs). The man's name was Carl Schneider. I remember him really well because he had a big pack of Juicy Fruit in his pocket, and every time he popped a piece into his mouth, he offered me one, too. I was following him around, piling supplies in his basket, and by the time we reached the cash register, my mouth was so full of gum, I could hardly speak. "What do you think, kid?" Mr. Schneider asked, stroking the kitten's orange fur. "Will she be happy with me?"

Two weeks later Mom pointed out an article on the front page of the newspaper. Mr. Schneider was part of a "Cleveland mob" responsible for drug trafficking and for the murders of three public officials, it said.

They also say Hitler was a vegetarian.

Guranga landed behind me. I've known her since I was a little kid, when she gave me my first Dr. Seuss story. She peered at the screen and shook her head sadly. "This may sound old-fashioned, Aaron," she said, "but why not try some books?"

Sharon Trout had asked me when I'd told her about my idea. Sharon's the one who taught me to surf, rather than stumble through, the Web. She's also the only person with whom I spend as much time as I do with animals.

It wasn't my idea to be such good friends with a girl, but she came to tutor me in math one day, and somehow, she just stuck.

"It's his work that interests me," I explained. "He pioneered studies in —"

"Why not pick someone like John F. Kennedy, or Mahatma Gandhi?" she interrupted.

She interrupts a lot!

"Done too often." I shrugged. I still don't know how to argue with her.

The Birdman wasn't just any murderer. In solitary confinement, he began to raise birds, then to study them with the same intensity with which he'd committed his crimes. He became a world expert on canaries.

It's weird how he could murder two men and yet like animals so much.

One time this guy came into our pet store and bought a kitten and about two-hundred-dollars' worth of supplies for it. My parents always introduce themselves and ask the customer's name. It's as if the people who come

◉ ◉ ◉ Guranga usually likes me to go with her when she's helping me research, so she can show me how books are shelved and stuff, but this time she flew away. I guess she decided I could stay on the Net a little while longer.

I clicked on the next site. There was a cartoon of Alcatraz island. It said: LAST RESORT. FREE TRANSPORTATION: ONE WAY.

Guranga returned with the books and set them on a nearby table. "I'll look for more," she said, and disappeared. I clicked on the cartoon, and a photo of Alcatraz appeared. It was like a giant factory of prisoners set on a floating rock. There were photographs of the cells, too. They were the size of walk-in closets, with a bed, a sink, and bars, of course. I logged off and went to the table to look at the books. In the couple of minutes since Guranga left them, some guy had plopped himself down in front of them like it was *his* report.

He was a big guy, about forty or so, with a rubbery face like a gorilla's. One arm rested on my stack of books, while the other held up a book close to his face, like he'd forgotten his glasses.

"Hi." I sat down at the table, trying to figure out a polite way to ask for my books.

"Are you talking to me?" He sounded pleased, like he was surprised that human beings could speak.

"Uh, yeah."

"You gotta love it," he said, setting the book down. I slid it toward me. One down and the four under his arm to go. "They didn't let him have birds there," he said.

"Huh?"

"At Alcatraz. They didn't let the Birdman have birds there. He had them at Leavenworth. So why do they call him the Birdman of Alcatraz?"

"I dunno." I hadn't done enough research to figure it out.

"Name's TB." He held out his hand.

"Aaron Betts." I shook it. "I'm writing a report on the Birdman of Alcatraz."

"Interested in criminals?"

"Animals. My family has a pet store."

"A pet store? You gotta love it. Used to work with elephants myself, in the circus, but then there was a little mishap. What's the name of the pet store?"

"Betts Pets." Business has been pretty slow the last couple of years; I always try to advertise our shop when I can.

"It rhymes! Isn't that cute. You ever read *Hocus Pocus*?"

"No."

"It's by Kurt Vonnegut. The very first page says, 'While there is a criminal element I am of it. While there is a soul in prison I am not free.'"

"Sounds good." I peered at the books under his arm. One of them was Stroud's book on canary diseases.

"Those words were on a tombstone. I only read that first page, then some guy got it from me and lit it on fire. I don't think it's right to burn books, do you?"

"No."

"They put him in solitary for that."

Solitary?

"They didn't care about the book, but arson is frowned upon in the Big House. Uh-oh." He leapt to his feet. "There's that librarian again. She's one scary broad. Thanks for saying hi to me; you're a good kid. I hope I can return the favor." He lumbered away.

"This'll do ya." Guranga plopped three more books in front of me.

chapter 3

◎ ◎ ◎ My mom is redecorating. When we first moved into the apartment above our shop, it was about as dusty as a used bookstore. A leaky roof had left the carpet completely mildewed and the floor beneath it stained. Red velvet wallpaper covered every wall, giving an eerie pink sheen to the room. As my mom put it when she walked in, "Gee, it looks like a house of ill repute."

Last week she enlisted a high school kid who had stopped to apply at our shop. Together they stripped the red velvet off and sanded the wood floors. Then, while I was at school, she found this wallpaper with pictures of palm trees, hibiscus, and little umbrellas like they serve in drinks at fancy hotels, and covered the walls. "We could be in Florida or Hawaii!" Mom chirped when I got home and practically keeled over from shock. It's January, and the snow the plow pushed up is piled in clumps along the sidewalks. "I'm getting futons and rat-tan furniture to make it inviting," Mom added quickly. "Should be delivered next week."

I think the sour look on my face made her feel pretty nervous, because she didn't ask me how I liked it like she normally would. "Now that we don't have a landlord, we can bring Toddy up occasionally. He'll feel right at home in this tropical setting," she added. Toddy is our myna bird. I sometimes bring him on Fridays, when I visit my friend Bertha in her nursing home. Bertha was the first person he ever talked to. He said, "Good morning, ma'am," to her, and she was delighted. He's gotten to be my favorite pet.

"Did you paper my room with this, too?"

"No, dear." She laughed. "Definitely not. You get to choose your own."

That made me feel better. I hang out in my own room a lot of the time, anyway, so I figured I could get used to living in Mom's "Florida" the rest of the time. "What we really need is an alligator to make it feel authentic," I joked.

"I'm so glad you like it! I hope your dad feels the same."
So she hadn't asked him.

"He may not even notice," I said encouragingly. It was probably true. My dad inhabits his own world, which mostly involves eating, sleeping, doing crossword puzzles, and playing poker.

X X X

Before we moved upstairs, I used to go straight to the pet store after school, but now I stop at home first. I have a snack and do my homework at the kitchen table. I used to have fried wontons for my snack, but when my skin started looking spotty, I switched to steamed dumplings.

The kitchen was still the same as when we moved in, although Mom had put a string across the back wall and hung up my drawings with clothespins. There are drawings of a polar bear, a rhesus monkey, and a bald eagle soaring over a mountain, plus some etchings I made of the construction of Cross Downs, luxury condominiums. I usually draw animals, but lately I've been experimenting more. Like I drew a picture of the empty storefront at the mall that will become Wong's Chinese and Italian Cuisine, then I drew Tony's dad putting up the sign.

Mom came in with her usual pile of papers. She put on the round black reading glasses that make her look like an owl. She teaches third grade and often grades her papers while I'm doing my homework.

When she first went back to teaching, she was a substitute. A couple of times she subbed at my school. I thought it would be cool, but it turned out to be pretty uncomfortable. The very first day she subbed, I was walking down the hall and I heard this really obnoxious kid, Brad Summers, say, "Hey, did you get a load of that sub? She looks like a bowling ball with glasses."

The other kids laughed. I thought about going over and punching Brad in the face; I guess that's what you're supposed to do when someone insults your mom, but luckily, Tony Wong picked just that moment to grab me and give me some bad news, news that actually took my mind off Brad Summers and my mom's round form.

"Guess what?" He didn't wait for me to guess. "We're moving our business to the mall."

I was stunned. Wong's Chinese Food is the only other business on our street. It's like we're the last holdouts in a war or something. My dad would call it the war on the little man. We eat there almost every day.

"When?" I asked.

"Don't worry," he said. "I'll still live across the street from your place. I know how you hate change."

"I do not hate change," I lied. *Since when did you start talking to me like a school counselor?* I thought.

When I looked back, Brad was gone.

X X X

Now my mom has her own classroom, but it's in a pretty tough school. "There was a fight in my class today." Mom laid her papers in stacks all over the table.

"Really?"

"That little boy, Tom Croaks..." She peered over her glasses. "His mom doesn't have him enrolled in free lunch. She insists on packing his lunch. So every day the poor kid shows up with his filthy Power Rangers lunch box. And all that's in it are Oreos, soda, and packaged peanut-butter crackers."

"Sounds okay to me."

"It's one hundred percent sugar! So it's no wonder he's all wound up."

"What happened?"

"We're working on Greek myths, and I handed out pictures with Medusa or Zeus. Well, Tom got a Zeus and

I guess he wanted Medusa — all those snakes coming out of her head and all — so he just grabbed Theo's sheet. Of course, he could've just asked to change. I had plenty of Medusas. Theo got upset, and, it turns out, he had a butter knife in his pocket. He pointed it at Tom and said, 'Come on, make my day!' I was busy helping another student, but when I heard that, I remembered it was from some violent movie. Arnold whatever-his-name-is, or Clint Eastwood. Now, why would an eight-year-old have watched such a film?"

"What did you do?"

"By the time I got over there, Tom's arms were working like a windmill. He wasn't actually connecting with Theo, he was just hitting at the air. Theo was staring at his butter knife. I took the knife. I could see what he was looking at. It was peanut butter, I think, all crusted onto the blade. So, I took it away, and brought them down to the office, and both of them were suspended."

"And these are third graders?"

"Of course. Who would think there could be such trouble over Greek gods? Life has certainly gotten exciting," she said in the singsong she uses when she's bummed out, "since I went back to teaching."

"Do you actually *like* teaching?"

"I do." She opened one of the fortune cookies. "It's just . . ."

"What?"

"Such problems with the children. Violence. And I miss being with your dad. Even now that I'm home, I have to stay up here and finish my grading. And frankly, I think he gets lonely."

"Why don't you grade down there? It's not like there'll be any customers to interrupt you."

"We're getting *more,*" Mom said. "People are coming in just to look at those wonderful birdcages Captain Blue has been making, especially after that nice article in the paper."

"Has anyone bought one yet?"

"No." She sighed and opened a fortune cookie. "'Irony loves company.' What kind of fortune is that?"

The Wongs change fortune-cookie companies more often than movie stars change their hairstyles.

"Mine says, 'I get no kick from champagne.'"

"That's a song."

"Do you *really* think Dad gets lonely?"

"Uh-huh, although Captain Blue does spend quite a lot of time there. The trouble is that when I go down there to grade, your dad has so much to tell me, I can't concentrate."

I'd noticed it, too. My dad's never been that talkative, but with my mom back to work, he spends most of the day in our pet shop by himself. Whenever he sees us, he talks up a storm.

"Oh well, I'll try to finish quickly." Mom leaned over her papers. She neatly corrected each spelling error and backward letter on the assignments about which Greek god the kids admired.

I took my plate to the sink and washed it, then wiped off the table. With Guranga's help, I'd gotten a good start on my paper and was going to go play with Tony Wong, but I decided to pay Dad a visit first.

I stopped in the living room. Even though it had been a week since the room makeover, it still felt foreign. It made me queasy inside, like I felt the first time I went on an airplane, as it lifted off the ground. I didn't know if it was the bright tropical colors or just change.

One thing hadn't changed, though. The box was still there. It was shoved under a small table: MOM AND DAD — MEMORABILIA, it said. It was a box Mom had gotten after her parents died in a car accident. As far as I knew, it's the only thing she had left from them, and she'd never opened it.

chapter 4

◎ ◎ ◎ I put my books away and took the "secret passageway" down to the shop. It's a stairway that leads from our kitchen to the storeroom of the pet shop. I was glad to see that Dad wasn't alone. Captain Blue, the older man who crafts fancy birdcages, was sitting on the stool next to him, and they were deep in conversation. Before my family moved upstairs, Captain Blue was using the apartment to get together with his girlfriend, Bertha. Bertha would've been his wife, but she was married to this mean rich man, and she and the Captain ran away from him. Now that Bertha's in a nursing home, the Captain hangs out in our shop.

I sat on the floor in the back of the shop and pulled out Larry, one of the guinea pigs. He climbed up my arm and sat on my shoulder, his whiskers twitching against my neck. Our cat, Twinkledoon, crept closer. I could tell that it took all his self-control not to pounce on Larry.

"So I told the man, 'I may have holes in my shoes . . .' " The Captain held up a foot. True to his word, he had two wide holes in the sole. " 'But I will never have holes in my pockets.' "

"That's a good story," my dad said.

"And a true one," the Captain replied. "Think about what can happen if you have holes in your pockets — the things that can spill out. Not just coins or postage stamps. Your very soul."

The word *soul* made me think of Guranga's conversation with the old lady.

Dad nodded his head seriously. He dug his hands into his pockets and pulled out a wrapper for snack cakes and one for a chocolate bar. Then he turned his pockets out and looked at them with dismay. Both pockets had holes. One was so big, he could poke his finger through it.

Captain Blue shook his head sadly. "My good man, you need new trousers!"

"You think?" Dad shoved the pockets back into his pants.

"When I was a boy, during the Depression, I wore the same pair of trousers for three years. They were practically shorts by the time I got new ones." Captain Blue laughed. "But the Depression is over."

"Coulda fooled me," Dad said grimly.

"History does repeat," the Captain joked.

I put Larry back into the cage with Curly and Mo and picked up Twinkledoon. He likes to wrap himself around my neck like a scarf. I walked to the front of the store.

"Aaron, my man!" Captain Blue held up his hand for a high-five.

"Today's your lucky day," Dad said. "It was so slow, I did all your chores."

I tried to look grateful, but I was kind of bummed. I like doing my pet-shop chores, and I hate to have my schedule thrown off. "Thanks, Dad."

"And today I sold all of the mice to a man who raises snakes in Evanston. He came all the way here to buy them."

"Great." It's the one sale that doesn't thrill me, selling the little guys to be dinner for snakes.

"How's Bertha?" I asked the Captain. Before I ever even met the Captain, I knew Bertha. She used to stand in the empty lot down the street that's now Cross Downs. Every day, on my way home, she'd stop me and tell me these jumbled nursery rhymes.

I wasn't allowed to visit her the past two Fridays because she had the flu. That threw me off even more than Dad doing my chores. I missed her.

"Not so good." He shook his head. "She's no longer sick, but her language has shrunk. She's just down to the titles of stories and rhymes. Maybe it's the loss of memory, but I'm worried she may be depressed."

I had thought there was something different the last time I'd seen her. Usually she recites nursery rhymes, with mixed-up words. Last time, though, she just kept staring out the window. It was like there was something dramatic going on out there, rather than just the last few leaves falling off the tree.

"Maybe she's just tired from being sick."

"Maybe so. Maybe so," the Captain said, but I could tell he didn't believe it.

Dad ruffled the pages of the newspaper. "There's a great big crossword here just waiting for our three brains. Thirteen-letter word that means 'to be reborn.'"

Weird!

chapter 5

◎ ◎ ◎ "You didn't!" Sharon shrieked over the phone line. I could just picture her pacing the room with her portable phone. I've seen her do it before. She has this little pink cordless that she carries around with her. One time I was over swimming, and her mom called from California. Her mom's a golf pro; she travels all the time. Sharon floated around on a raft with her pink phone, talking away about putting tees and golf greens.

Our phone is a big black beast with a rotary dial. If I call one of those numbers where you have to press this or that to get to the next step, I'm out of luck. You have to stand at the kitchen counter to call anyone.

I probably wouldn't have mentioned the weird guy at the library if I hadn't been so worn out. Tony and I had played soccer for three hours straight. We fell into the banks of snow lots of times. By the time we were finished, we were practically frostbitten.

"It's no big deal."

"You gave your full name, and the store's, to some criminal? That is a very big deal. Didn't your mom tell you not to speak to strangers?" Sharon could make a drama out of a raindrop.

"I don't know if he was an ex-convict."

"Well, the Big House is hardly a mansion. Did he give you *his* name?"

"TB."

"That's a disease."

"Whatever. Just don't make a federal case out of it."

"Oh, a pun. Goody. Shall I come over?"

"It's kind of late. Let's get together tomorrow."

"I'll have Loafer bring me after my saxophone class."

"I thought it was viola."

"I switched."

Loafer is Sharon's chauffeur and sort-of babysitter. Last summer he fell in love with a French tourist and followed her to Paris.

"When did Loafer get back?"

"Last week," Sharon said, "but he's not in a very good mood. He spent all the money he saved, then the girl told him she had a fiancé."

"I can see why he's in a bad mood."

"It's not just that. He decided that he's meant to be a poet, and he says poets have to be miserable in order to create. So now he says all these dark things like, 'Existence is without reason,' 'Nothingness, *rien.*'"

"What does *rien* mean?"

"That's also 'nothingness,' only in French. But at least he's back, so I'm getting places. My mom always promises she'll drive me, then she gets too booked up with social events."

"Do you think he can drive us to the mall next Saturday? Wong's is having their grand opening."

"Sure. There's some pajamas I want at The Limited."

After I hung up I wondered what I'd gotten myself into. Looking for girls' pajamas is not exactly my idea of fun. I get enough flak as it is for being friends with Sharon Trout, without being seen in a girlie store.

It was just about dark. The last bit of light was floating at the top of the sky like some kind of space ship. It's eerie the way dark comes on, so slowly at first, and then suddenly. I thought about the Birdman of Alcatraz. What would it be like to have only a window to the world for most of the day?

Mom came into the kitchen. She started arranging some of my drawings. "This is one of your best." She held up a drawing of Jacobs Field. "I like the way the stadium dwarfs the people. It's an unusual perspective. Oh, here's ten dollars. Our order should be ready at Wong's. Could you run over and pick it up?"

"Sure."

I opened the door and dashed out onto the landing, practically tripping over a box in front of our door. It wasn't sealed, and there was nothing written on it. But inside, I could hear a scratching noise. Something was moving in the box.

chapter 6

◎ ◎ ◎ I tugged on the top flap a little. Whatever it was, I didn't want it jumping out at me. I opened the door to our apartment wider to add some light to the dark landing. Then slowly I opened the other flap.

It was a small turtle making its snail-like way across the box. On the turtle's shell, someone had painted an elaborate design in pink, green, and yellow.

There's a species of turtle called a map turtle, and also one called a painted turtle, but these colors were nothing like you'd see in nature. They reminded me of rainbow sherbet.

I looked around. I'd heard about people dropping babies on the steps of orphanages; could someone have left the turtle in front of our door? And why not leave it at the pet shop?

I picked the turtle up and examined the shell. The design was so intricate that I'd have to look at it under a magnifying glass to really see the detail. I brought him inside.

"Look what I found." I held out the turtle to Mom.

"Is it one of ours?"

"No."

"I'm not happy about that paint." Mom peered through her round glasses at the bright paint.

"Yeah, who would do something like that?"

"Some third grader," she joked. "It can't be good for him. Well, at least you'll have someone to keep you company tonight."

"Where are you going?"

"Your dad doesn't know it yet, but we're going to Weight Watchers."

"'Weight Watchers'?"

"Uh-huh. You may not have noticed, but your dad and I have been expanding pretty steadily the last few years. Too many sweets and fried foods, I guess. And his cholesterol is through the roof. So we're going to do this." She went to a kitchen cupboard and pulled a little scale out of a white box. "From now on we'll be weighing our food."

"Even me?"

"No, not you, dear. You're skinny as a rail." Mom pulled out a couple of charts and taped them on the wall next to the scale. "Your dad is in for a surprise."

"Let's weigh the turtle."

"Better not. I'm going to put food on this. That turtle could carry salmonella. And wash your hands with hot water and soap after you set up his habitat. There are some empty aquariums in the storage room. Maybe we should take him to the vet. He doesn't look too healthy."

"How can you tell?"

"Look at his eyes. They're dull. And his head movements. Lethargic."

"Yeah. I see what you mean. So we won't sell him?"

"Definitely not. We don't know his history or his health. He looks smaller than the four-inch minimum size, as well. I'd better get moving. Don't want to be late for the first meeting."

"But why do you go to a meeting if you have all these charts and stuff?"

"Just to talk about food and dieting. For support."

Boy, did that sound boring. I could just picture my dad snoring away.

"What are you going to name him?" she asked.

"Huh?"

"The turtle."

"Birdman."

"You never disappoint. Every name is unusual. But where's your dinner from Wong's?"

"Oh."

"Never mind. I'll have your dad get it. You just do something about that sick turtle."

She patted my cheek and rushed out. I looked at her charts. The first one was a description of "points." It listed the foods you could eat and their nutrition and stuff. The second one was a series of menus: BREAK-FAST: ½ GRAPEFRUIT, ½ CUP COTTAGE CHEESE, 3 MELBA TOASTS. I didn't know what a Melba toast was, but I could guess by the other two items that it probably didn't have much flavor. LUNCH: ½ CUP SALAD GREENS WITH FRESH LEMON JUICE, 4-½ OUNCES BROILED CHICKEN, ½ BAKED POTATO WITH 2 TBS. COTTAGE CHEESE, 8 OUNCES SKIM MILK.

I went downstairs and got the supplies and set up the aquarium. I added a bit of canned dog food to the turtle's food, hoping it would perk him up. I set him next to me where I could observe him.

It's funny but I'm rarely ever apart from my parents, aside from going to school. There are a lot of kids, like Sharon, whose parents have big careers and are so busy, the kids hardly ever see them, but not me. I spent all of my first five years in the pet store with my parents, then every day after school, and summers. It was odd to be in the apartment alone.

I sat in front of the TV and flipped through the channels. Two sumo wrestlers were stuck together like rams locking horns. They were twisting and turning, but it seemed like the camera always focused on their bare butts in those diaper things. It would've been funny to watch with someone. I flipped again. A really old nun was making jokes about all the medication she took. She talked to God, she said, but the patches she was supposed to put on her skin for heart disease still stuck on everything but her. I flipped again. On the next three channels, some guy was chasing another guy with a gun. I flipped again and again and got commercial after commercial, including a show that was just one long commercial where ladies talked about how soft their skin was as if they were solving world hunger.

I always go through every channel and stop to listen to a bit of each show. It drives my mom crazy. My dad and I have battles over who gets control of the flipper, which actually end up being more fun than watching TV. Like we'll arm wrestle, or flip coins, or bet on games of poker, and by the time we've matched and rematched, we've forgotten all about the TV.

Finally, I turned off the set. The apartment was so quiet I could hear my own breath. Even the windows, which make a whistling sound at the slightest breeze, were silent. Before my family moved in, Sharon and I did a stakeout up here. That night, every wall seemed to creak or moan. That was how we met the Captain.

I pulled out my art supplies. Last year my teacher, Mrs. Felty, gave me a book called *The Intuitive Artist*. It has all kinds of art exercises for "reaching the inner artist," like drawing with your eyes closed, or with your left hand, or visualizing a scene and then drawing as fast as you can.

It's a cool book. I use the exercises in it all the time. And it pleased me that Mrs. Felty, who had been nagging me all year about drawing in class when I was supposed to be studying, actually thought my work was interesting.

I took Birdman into my room and set him on the rug.

He stuck out his head and looked slowly around like he was surveying his new digs. It was hard to tell if he liked what he saw.

I pulled out some newsprint and charcoal. I'm trying to do a couple of exercises each day. Now I did one where you close your eyes and keep the pencil moving without lifting it from the page. When I was done, I looked and found I'd made a pretty decent picture of a cyclone and a town. The cyclone was just lifting a building off the ground, sort of like Dorothy's house in *The Wizard of Oz*.

They say that ducks waddle, but I'll tell you, turtles waddle, too. Birdman waddled slowly over to my drawing and peered down at it. I got out my magnifying glass and examined his shell again.

The painting on his shell was very precise. I took out my colored pencils and drew Birdman, taking care to get every detail of his shell just right.

Then I duplicated just the shell part and enlarged it. The lines ran in a grid: yellow one way, and pink and lime green the other. There were curving lines, too, especially in the middle — black lines in a whorl like the shell of a snail. Without the turtle's body and head, the drawing looked a whole lot like a map.

chapter 7

◎ ◎ ◎ Our teacher is pregnant. There's nothing weird about that, unless you're trying to walk up the aisle the same time she is and she makes one of her sudden turns and knocks into you. It's like trying to pass a whale in a tight canal.

The weird part is that she never said anything to us about it. She just got bigger and bigger. Kids started joking in that way they do (in the way they did about my mom) about her eating habits, but soon the shape became very obvious. There were more whispers until finally Mick Fromer, a kid who looks and acts like a baboon, said, "Are you pregnant, or something, Mrs. Gaps?"

Mrs. Gaps is just OK as teachers go. She's got this face with about three different expressions: spaced out, worried, and mad. She reminds me of a groundhog somehow, a pregnant groundhog, although I definitely wouldn't tell her that because she has no sense of humor. Absolutely zero.

At Mick's question Mrs. Gaps went through all three of her expressions, landing on mad. "'Or *something*'?" she said.

"Well, you just look like you're going to have a baby any second."

"Of course I'm *expecting*. I'm at seven and a half months, to be exact, so you can see that the baby is not going to come 'any second.' Surely I mentioned it to you at the beginning of the year."

We all looked around at one another. A couple of the girls, including Sharon Trout, shook their heads.

"No?" Mrs. Gaps said. "Well, this is my third, after all. I guess it's just lost its novelty this time around."

X X X

After school I waited outside for Sharon to finish her detention for mouthing off about the food to the cafeteria lady. I could see Loafer across the street, waiting in the car. He had a notebook on the steering wheel, and he was staring at it, like he expected it to tell him something. I didn't want to disturb his concentration, but it was freezing cold, so I got in the car.

"Aaron!" He turned around. "Long time no see."

"I didn't want to interrupt your work," I said. "Sharon told me you're writing poetry now."

Loafer held up the blank notebook. "I have a feeling that if I could just write the first word, even if it was *the*, that the rest would come pouring out. Ya know, it's like some kid has his finger in the faucet."

"Why don't you just write *the?*"

Loafer flipped to the previous page. The word *the* was written on it about a hundred times. He flipped to another page. The word *love* was written on it; he tapped the word. "Now that's a tough one because people think there's only one kind of love, when there's really about one million. I discovered that in Paris. As many kinds of love as shades of light."

Now, that *is a good line,* I thought. "What did you do while you were there?"

"Walked mostly. The Left Bank. The Right. The one in between. Museums. Cafés. I was looking for art, for inspiration. I hoped to see the little short guy who painted all those posters of women dancing . . ."

"Who?"

"You know. The famous one. Moulin Rouge and all that."

"Toulouse-Lautrec?"

"Uh-huh."

"But he's dead."

"I know. I know." Loafer nodded his head sadly. "I wrote a poem about him when I was in Paris, but then I lost it. The first line was 'Toulouse. Toulouse. You were so short, but your paintbrush was tall.'"

"Sounds good."

"It wasn't," he said mournfully, "but it beats *the*."

"Well, you can find inspiration in Cleveland."

"Maybe in the old factories or the seedy side of town. But I doubt it. What I've learned is that you should decide early on what you want to be. Like you. You're young. Do you know what you want to be?"

"A zoologist, or an artist," I said.

He clutched his hand to his heart. "Comrade! An artist! You know how misguided I was? I wanted to be an air-traffic controller, not a poet. Just stand on that runway and wave my arms, watch those tiny landing planes grow bigger and bigger until they're right on top of me, like some dream — I say stuff like that now that I'm a poet. And stuff like this: 'Nothingness is a vine around my bed. Nothingness is a blue ball in my head.' I said that to the mailman this morning, and he turned and ran, like I was nuts. The other thing I wanted to be was a kung fu master, like that guy on the TV show, one of those Carradine brothers — just go around and help out if anyone got into trouble. I studied kung fu for eight years, but I never found anyone in trouble. And I never ever applied for an air-traffic controller's job."

"That's too bad."

"Of all the indignities!" Sharon opened the door and slammed into her seat. "Do you know what Mr. Medlicott made me do in detention? Clean the chalkboards. Like I was a slave or something, a character in some archaic novel. I'm surprised he didn't strike my hand with a ruler."

"Were they dirty?" I asked.

"My hands?"

"The chalkboards!"

"Filthy! And I coughed and sneezed and told him about my allergies."

"I thought you didn't have allergies."

"Well, I do now. I told Medlicott, and you know what he did? He said that *he* was allergic. Wait till I tell my father."

I didn't say anything, because I could see Sharon was in one of those moods where she reminds me of some spoiled character from TV: Muffy Crosswire from *Arthur*, or one of those girls who say "Scandalous!" on *Recess*.

"That doesn't sound so bad," Loafer made the mistake of saying. "Cleaning a couple of chalkboards."

"Why isn't this car moving?" Sharon snapped. "Not that I could tell if you *were* driving; you drive like a snail."

Loafer turned the key in the ignition. I could tell from the way he shoved his cap on that his feelings were hurt. I gave Sharon a dirty look, but she was too busy being mad to notice.

"It's a lot easier for me to drive when you actually tell me where we're going."

"We're going to Aaron's place," Sharon instructed.

"Okay . . . brat," Loafer said. I felt better after that because Loafer was holding his own.

"Drive past Cross Downs," Sharon demanded.

"Why are you obsessed with that place, Mademoiselle Trout?"

"That's a new word for you, Loafer . . . *obsessed* . . . ,"
Sharon said. "But I guess it beats *brat*."

"I call 'em as I see 'em."

Sharon sighed. It was like she was a balloon releasing
her hot air. She doesn't usually stay mad for long. "Cross
Downs is cool 'cause it's always changing, being added
on to. It's like this play town I had as a kid, and every
week Mom would buy me a new piece so I could add a
barbershop or a church, or something. So, what are you
writing about lately, Loafer?"

"Obsession."

"Why don't you read us one of your poems?"

"So you can make fun of me?"

"I wouldn't do that," she said, and she sounded sin-
cere.

"Language has become everything to me. Even the
word *the* has new meaning."

I hoped he wasn't going to show her that page. Then
she *would* laugh her head off.

"You should meet Bertha. Shouldn't he, Aaron?"

"Uh-huh."

"Bertha does all kinds of cool things with language."

"That the one at the nursing home?" Loafer asked.

"Uh-huh." Sharon nodded. "She's a kind of poet

savant, or something like that. She takes nursery rhymes and twists the words. Next time we visit, you come in, too."

"Okay." Loafer sounded cheerful. I'll bet he doesn't get invited to do much.

It made me feel kind of sick to my stomach to talk about Bertha, though. The doctor had told Captain Blue that she shouldn't have any visitors this week, either — "any *excitement*" was how he put it. It made me wonder if I'd *ever* see her. And even if I did, would she still know me and be happy to see me?

"Cross Downs." Loafer pulled up to the curb. The revolving doors of Cross Downs moved in a continuous circle. Just above the doors was that terrible sign, the one that had dashed my family's hopes when the new condominiums opened: NO PETS.

"We'll walk from here, Loafer. Pick us up at Betts Pets in an hour and a half," Sharon said.

"I'm gonna follow, to make sure you get there safely."

"Suit yourself." Sharon sniffed as we stepped out of the car. "This place is really hopping. What are they building there?"

"I think it's going to be a bar," I said. On the lower level of Cross Downs was a weird concrete addition. It had been "under construction" for about the last three months, but I never saw anyone working on it. The windows were covered in black plastic, like some badly wrapped present. Yellow CAUTION tape was drawn all across the front of it. For some reason, it gave me the creeps.

"Do you still count your steps?" Sharon asked.

"Who told you that?"

"Tony."

Great. I decided not to answer, because the truth is, I still do count my steps. It makes me feel comfortable, like at least there's one thing that hasn't changed.

"What would you do if your parents had something that was sort of secret and you kind of wanted to know about it?" I asked.

"Speak English! What are you talking about?"

"Never mind."

"No, really," she said more softly.

"My mom has this box of stuff from her parents, and she never seems to want to open it."

"You mean that old box under the table?"

"Uh-huh."

"It's probably just junk."

"Yeah."

"I'd just open it if I were you."

I tried to imagine what would be in it: old photographs — that would be cool — baby clothes, letters? It was odd, but every time I asked Mom to open it, she found some excuse not to.

We reached Betts Pets. The sign had just been redone in red and black. Captain Blue had painted a bright parrot on the window. A row of his handmade birdcages graced one shelf. If our shop were in the mall, people would take one look at the beautiful cages and come in. The store looked nicer than it had in years, and emptier.

"By the way, don't mention the talking-to-strangers thing to my mom."

"Do I look like a moron?"

"Hi, Sharon," Toddy said as we walked into the room. He's the smartest myna bird we've ever had. I thought about the reincarnation lady in the library. Could humans be reborn as animals? And if so, was that a step up, or down?

Sharon and I have gotten into a routine. She takes the right side of the shop where the hamsters, gerbils, and bunnies are, and I take the left, with the reptiles. There are different chores each day. Today was the easiest day;

all we had to do was feed them. It only took twenty minutes.

We went upstairs. It was the first time Sharon had been in since Mom's redecorating. She looked around the room, her eyes widening. "Wow, Mrs. Betts," Sharon said, "this is so cool!"

Mom was measuring some carrots on the scale. She carefully laid them out on two plates, next to a scoop of cottage cheese and some celery sticks. "Your dumplings are in the microwave," she said. "There's plenty for Sharon."

"I'll have some of those Melba toasts," Sharon purred. "I love those."

"Here you go, Sharon. Would you like a peach half?"

"Yes, please. Are you reducing, Mrs. Betts?"

"We are trying, Sharon. I even bought his-and-hers running shoes so we can start exercising." Mom pointed to two shoeboxes. "We still haven't used them."

"I certainly admire your fortitude," Sharon said. She says dumb stuff like that to adults. "I once lost five pounds on a grapefruit diet, but it crept right back on again."

I pulled Birdman out of his aquarium. The paint hadn't faded a bit.

"You don't need to lose weight," Mom said.

Sharon smiled; it was just what she was fishing for. I put down newspaper and laid Birdman on the table. His head was out but it was droopy, lifeless. It reminded me of a dog who'd been running around in the heat. "Mom?"

She read my mind. "No. He doesn't look good at all. I wonder what they used when they painted his shell. I hope it didn't poison him."

"Wow," Sharon said. "It sure is pretty. It reminds me of a thumbprint, or a map."

"It does." Mom picked up the diet plates and went downstairs.

"There *is* such a thing as a map turtle," I explained. "*Graptemys kohnii.* There's even a painted turtle, *Chrysemys picta,* but this isn't either."

"Yech." Sharon wrinkled up her nose. "Those sound like infectious diseases."

I put Birdman on the floor. He waddled forward a step, then stopped. If he were a dog, I'd have said he was hanging his head.

"Looks like we have another mystery," Sharon said, "like when someone was stealing your pets and we had a stakeout and caught the criminal."

"That was just Captain Blue."

"Still, it was exciting."

I had to admit it was. "Nothing exciting here," I said. "Just one sick turtle."

"Yeah." She pushed her plate away and absently opened the box of running shoes. "Nike. Boy, your dad must have big feet. Hey!"

"What?"

Sharon handed me my dad's new running shoes. Inside each shoe was a bag of potato chips. "That's some diet," she said.

chapter 8

◎ ◎ ◎ Right after school on Thursday, I rushed home. I wanted to see if Bertha was better and we could visit. The Captain wasn't there, and I would've asked Dad about Bertha, but there was actually a customer. He wore a beige suit and was so tall that he had to duck his head a couple of times when he moved from room to room. He had a long neck and freckles. He reminded me of a giraffe.

I filled out a slip for three dollars so I could get money out of the cash register to go to Wong's. It was their last day in business across the street, which was almost enough to make me lose my appetite.

I punched in NO SALE, and the drawer started to fly open, but then it got stuck. When I pried it open, I realized the problem. Where the twenties and tens go, Dad had stuffed in a Mars bar and a couple of Snickers.

Dad shrugged. "A person could starve around here."

The customer had finally stopped his circling. He was looking carefully at the parakeets in their cage. "There are all kinds of prisons," he said.

That reminded me of the weird guy in the library, the lines he said from that book.

"Yeah." Dad pounced, happy to have an opening. "Some are necessary. These guys wouldn't last two seconds in the real world. Look at that turquoise one. Have you ever seen a parakeet that color? Reminds me of the stones in the Indian Museum. There was an ancient necklace —"

"Actually" — the man craned his long neck toward Dad — "what I'm looking for is a turtle."

chapter 9

◎ ◎ ◎   All the way to Wong's I wondered whether the Giraffe might be the one who'd actually lost Birdman. And if so, why didn't he just ask for him? I'd check it out when I got back.

Business had picked up in Wong's since Cross Downs was built; I still didn't get why they were moving to the mall. Today, though, there was only one customer, a guy in a ski cap. He was eating chow mein with a spoon, and more of it was spilling than getting in his mouth. He had enormous teeth, this guy. He reminded me of a beaver. When he noticed me looking at him, he picked up a newspaper and held it in front of his face.

"Aaron!" Tony's mom called out to me. She's one of the nicest people I know. She's also pretty. No one would call her a bowling ball. "I'm so glad to see you. Look at all this food. You must take it off my hands!" Mrs. Wong had loaded all the leftover food into white containers and lined them up on a tray.

I wondered if I should tell her about my parents' diet, but it didn't seem polite. "I don't know if we could eat all that, Mrs. Wong."

"It'll keep in the freezer." She smiled and shoved the tray across the counter.

"Thanks." I took the tray, and I was about to go when I noticed that Mrs. Wong was crying.

"Are you okay, Mrs. Wong?"

"I'm so silly." She laughed and wiped her eyes with her apron. "Just feeling sad about leaving this old shop."

"But you *are* staying upstairs?" I just had to ask again.

"Oh yes. And we're going to expand down here for Uncle Pow and Aunt Rita. Plus, I'm going to add Italian dishes to the new Wong's menu so I can really show my stuff." She had stopped crying and now she actually seemed happy. "Are you coming to the opening? It's a week from Saturday. That's where everyone is now. Last-minute preparations."

"I wouldn't miss it," I said.

By the time I got back to Betts Pets, the Giraffe was gone. Dad was sitting on his usual stool, eating the Mars bar.

"Wow, Aaron, I thought you were just after dumplings."

"Mrs. Wong gave me all this."

"Fantastic!" Dad rubbed his hands together. "A feast."

"I don't know if Mom will approve."

"We'll eat it before she gets home."

I wanted to tell Dad that it probably wasn't a good idea to cheat on his diet, but he looked too happy. "So what did the guy buy?" I asked.

"That man? He was a strange one. He made me take out every single turtle, then he stormed out of here and didn't buy a thing."

"Did you tell him about Birdman?"

"Birdman? Who's that?"

"My turtle, upstairs."

"No. Why should I? He's not for sale."

chapter 10

◎ ◎ ◎   Friday morning stunk. The pipe to the radiator burst, so the whole heating system was off. I hopped across the freezing floor and got dressed as quickly as possible. Mom called for a sub and sat at the table, leaving messages for one repairman after another. "Take the turtle," she hollered as I ran to catch the bus. "You don't want him to freeze here."

I knew I should leave him with Dad — there was still heat downstairs — but I really felt like he was *my* pet now. All I needed was for Dad to get forgetful and sell him to someone. Who knows? Maybe the Giraffe would come back. So I brought him into Mrs. Felty's class. Luckily, she got all excited by his painted shell and agreed to baby-sit him for the day, in one of her terrariums. Then she spent five minutes telling me about her upcoming wedding, so I was late to class.

Around ten the snow started. In contrast to the heating system at my house, the school's worked *too* well. Outside snow piled up. Inside we might as well have been in Tahiti. I hoped for the announcement that school would be closing, but no such luck. During math, I dozed off. I must've drooled, or something, because when I opened my eyes, half the class was smirking at me.

Since Mom had stayed home, she picked me up from school. We drove home at about five miles per hour on the icy roads, and I knew that even if something had changed and we were now allowed to visit Bertha, we weren't going anywhere. It made me feel kind of sick inside, like I was ignoring her, even if it wasn't my fault.

"Is the radiator fixed?" I asked.

"Uh-huh." We pulled up to Betts Pets. "Captain Blue fixed it. He's a wonder."

When I went upstairs to put Birdman away, I could see that his aquarium was lying on its side, the water in it dripping down my dresser onto the floor. Two of my drawers were open. It was creepy, but I figured maybe the Captain had to get in here to fix the plumbing or something.

I straightened things up and put Birdman back; he looked happy to be home. Then I went outside to check out the snow. Across the street was what Tony calls the Troutmobile, Sharon's mom's Mercedes SUV. I could see Sharon and Loafer arguing in the car.

Sharon rolled down the window. "Sorry I'm late, Aaron. Loafer got inspired and was an hour late to pick me up!"

I didn't even know she was coming.

"You said four o'clock," Loafer argued. "I was early. It had nothing to do with inspiration."

"I said *three*."

"Time is a galloping horse," Loafer said.

"Fine. Fine," Sharon barked. "Just come back in an hour. Mom's away and Dad will have a conniption if I'm late to dinner; he hates to eat alone."

"Fine," Loafer snapped. He sat in the car.

"Are you just going to sit there and freeze?" Sharon asked. "Go do something."

"I might get stuck in traffic." Loafer pouted. "I'd hate to be late."

"Why don't you come in and look at our animals?" I suggested.

Loafer hesitated. "Miss Trout won't like it."

"Sure. Come on, Loafer," Sharon said.

He followed us inside. The Captain and my dad were sitting at the counter, playing poker. They were so intent on what they were doing, they hardly noticed us.

"Cool place," Loafer said.

"Aaron's drawn every animal in this store," Sharon bragged.

"Very cool, my man." Loafer stopped in front of one of the Captain's cages. It takes Captain Blue a month of constant work to build one cage. He sculpts them out of copper wire and all kinds of cool stuff he finds at the dump. The one Loafer was looking at had a silver rim with bits of broken glass shaped like sails embedded in it.

"Now this," Loafer said, "is poetry."

"A fan!" the Captain said, rushing over. "I pried those strange pieces of glass off a hand mirror I found. A beautiful woman probably watched herself grow old in it."

"Loafer," Sharon said, "this is Captain Blue and Mr. Betts."

"Good to meet you," Dad said.

"I'm the young lady's chauffeur," Loafer responded.

"How 'bout joining us in a game of poker?" the Captain asked.

Loafer smiled. "Can't say I'd refuse."

X X X

Sharon followed me upstairs. "What's that line from that old Bogart film? Something about the beginning of a beautiful friendship?"

"Huh?"

"*Casablanca*," she said in that "*Duh*" tone of voice. "You know. At the end, when Humphrey Bogart and Claude Rains go off together?"

"Whatever." I learned that one from her. If you don't know something, you can just act like you're above it by saying "Whatever."

"I meant . . . it's nice that Loafer can be friends with your dad and the Captain. It'll keep him out of my hair, at least."

Having someone around to drive you places when you wanted didn't seem like having someone in your hair, but I let it go. I've learned not to argue with her. And yeah, it *was* nice to see him look happy for once.

"So, what should we do?" she asked.

We go through this all the time. With Tony Wong and me, we end up outside — crashing a ball around, any ball: soccerball, baseball, basketball. Sharon, half the time, says she just wants to *talk*. What's up with that?

"Let's see what Tony's up to."

"Translation:" — she frowned — "I watch you and Tony play sports or talk about sports."

"Well, we can play a game, then."

"No. It's okay. I'll go see the gross-out king, as long as we don't play sports."

"It's too cold to play anything."

"And we don't *talk* about sports."

"Deal."

"By the way, did your mom ever let you open that box?"

In answer I pointed to it on the way out. It was still there, taped up, hiding under the table like some unwanted kid.

X   X   X

Tony wasn't home, and it was depressing to see the storefront empty, even if it *was* going to be turned into an apartment.

"Does he still live there?" Sharon asked.

"Huh?"

"You should strike that word from your vocabulary. It's not even a word."

I feel like I'd like to strike *her* from my vocabulary sometimes. "He's never home, since they started that move to the mall. They even work late at night, and he has to do his homework there and everything."

Sharon didn't say anything. She was looking straight up at the sky. It was the color of dull metal. "That bird is acting strange," she said.

"What bird?" I looked up. A pigeon was circling above. At first there didn't seem anything odd about it, but as it descended, the circles got smaller and tighter.

"You ever see that old Hitchcock movie where all the birds go crazy and peck out people's eyes?" Sharon asked.

"Uh, no."

"I hope it doesn't poop on us. One time my dad was looking up to point to the Eiffel Tower and a pigeon pooped right on the lens of his glasses."

"Good thing he had glasses on."

The pigeon swooped down toward us, then away.

"Pigeons are so ordinary," Sharon complained.

"Passenger pigeons were once 'ordinary.' Now they're

extinct. The last one on earth died in 1914, in the Cincinnati Zoo."

"Why?"

"Hunting. Destruction of the habitat."

"Wow, that's really sad."

Softly, the pigeon alighted on the sidewalk. It had beautiful white-and-gray wings that seemed iridescent.

"I think it's a *homing* pigeon." I took a step toward it. The pigeon lifted off again and hovered above us.

"How can you tell?"

"The tag on its leg, and its appearance. In fact, it's got something on both legs. Maybe it has a message."

"Isn't it *carrier* pigeons who take messages?"

"Both can carry messages," I explained.

"The tag on its leg probably says: 'Made in Taiwan.'"

"Talk softly," I said. "I think it's going to land again."

"How do they find their way?"

"They're guided by the sun, by their senses, and by the lines of the earth's magnetic field. That's what scientists think, anyway. No one's really sure. A couple of years ago, thousands of pigeons from all over the place disappeared during a race, and never turned up again."

"Weird."

The pigeon landed next to me. I put out my hand. "It

was weird, because the weather was perfectly clear, and they were released from all over the place —"

"I'm freezing. Let's go in."

I felt the light prick of its claws on my forearm. I brought the other hand around and held it. Its body felt all quivery, like it was charged with electricity. On one leg was the permanent tag, the owner's claim to the bird. On the other was the message, in a small tube. I opened the tube. The message came out easily, but it was sticky and hard to unroll.

"Give it to me." Sharon grabbed it. "Boys are so clumsy with their hands."

Its duty fulfilled, the pigeon lifted off. It landed on the telephone line, then lingered as if it were uneasy about Sharon having the message. When I looked back at Sharon, her eyes and mouth were wide open. "Is this some kind of a joke, Aaron?"

"What?"

"I mean . . . you're pulling my leg. That's your bird, isn't it?"

"No."

She handed me the little piece of paper. The print was so small it took me a second to read it.

"It's no joke." I felt like the blood had frozen in my veins.

"What a nasty bird."

"Don't shoot the messenger," I said, trying to lighten things up with the old cliché.

The paper was the size of a fortune. In block letters, it read: GIV BAK MY TERTLE OR SUFER.

chapter 11

◉ ◉ ◉ Lately Mrs. Gaps seems to be slipping. She sits at her desk, hiding yawns behind her hand. A couple of times I've seen her nod off. And it takes her forever to get work back to us.

"Here are your biography papers." She finally handed back our papers. "They didn't get swept away in the ocean."

I'd worked hard on the Birdman of Alcatraz paper, and my heart sank when I looked at the grade: C. Then I realized she'd given me Tony's paper. His was on Babe Ruth, and I could see it was short. Tony walked over and handed me mine.

"Thanks," I said.

He looked at his new grade. "Maybe I'll keep yours."

On my paper, in her scrawling handwriting, Mrs. Gaps had written: *Compelling reading* — A. A nice compliment, even if she thought I was Tony. I reread my paper. It *was* good. I'd wanted to focus on Robert Stroud's work on canaries, but more and more I found myself writing about his personality. Did he become a criminal because he had a mean dad and a difficult childhood? Or was it just something inside of him, some craziness?

On the last page, I'd drawn a pretty good picture of Stroud when he was older, after he'd left Alcatraz. Stroud looked like a bird — but not like a canary. He looked like a hawk.

X   X   X

Walking to lunch, Tony caught up with me. "The business is really hurting my grades," he said. "I don't have time for anything, not even basketball."

"Maybe you can talk to your parents about it," I suggested. Tony was like Sharon. He was used to getting As.

I took my packed lunch to the table. Before I could tell her that I was saving a place for Tony, who'd stopped to talk to the coach about missing practice, Sharon plopped down beside me.

"I left my lunch in the car, so I have to have school *blech*. What is this thing on my plate?"

"A cupcake with peanut butter frosting."

"It's like we're four-year-olds or something, the food they give us. I'm surprised there's no colored sprinkles."

"You sure like to complain."

"It's the universal language." Sharon yawned. "That's what my mom says. Anyway, I've been thinking."

"Uh-oh."

"This pigeon thing must have to do with that ex-con you were talking to at the library. Who else would be sending threatening birds?"

"It was the note that was threatening, not the bird."

"Same thing."

"We don't even know if he was an ex-con."

"One thing for sure —" She bit into the cupcake.

"What?" I asked reluctantly.

"We're not giving anyone that turtle."

X   X   X

I appreciated Sharon's determination, but it ended up being a moot point. When I got home from school,

Mom was already there, standing in the kitchen with a worried look on her face.

"Hi, Mom."

"Hello, Aaron."

"What's up?"

"I brought Toddy upstairs."

"Great."

"He's in your bedroom."

Something about Mom's tone made me realize I wasn't getting the full story.

"With Birdman?" I asked hopefully.

"Well," Mom started, but I didn't wait for the answer. I dashed into my room and looked in the aquarium. It was empty. Mom followed me in.

"Was he stolen?"

"Why would anyone steal a turtle?"

That made me feel a little guilty. I should've told her about the pigeon, the Giraffe, and everything. "What happened?"

"He died. I thought he would. I'm sorry, Aaron. I should've waited for you to get home because, well, this wasn't like the pets in the store; this was *your* pet. It's just, I know you don't like to see dead animals, if it's possible . . ."

"Oh . . ." I'd finally gotten it.

"I gave him a burial at sea," she continued. "I hope you're not too mad that I didn't wait for you. I mean, maybe you would've wanted to really bury him, although the ground is pretty frozen."

"A burial at sea" means being flushed down the toilet. When you have as many animals as we do, death loses its formality.

"No, Mom," I said slowly. "It's okay."

"I should've waited. I was worried about diseases and contagions. It was kind of awful, because he didn't go down easily. He got stuck the first couple of flushes and I had to get the plunger. I just wasn't thinking . . ."

"It's okay," I repeated, but I didn't really mean it. Maybe I've just gotten to the age where I want to say goodbye to things rather than being afraid to see something that was once alive be completely still. "Are you going to Weight Watchers tonight?"

"We don't have to . . ."

"Go ahead," I said. "I'll be fine. I've got a ton of homework."

"Go ahead. Go ahead," Toddy mimicked. I took him out of the cage. He hopped onto my shoulder, which made me feel better. And at least the turtle drama was over.

chapter 12

◎ ◎ ◎ On Saturday Loafer drove us to the mall. I felt kind of bummed; the last couple of times I'd come here had been with Bertha. We'd had a great time. The Captain and I had walked around with her, window-shopping and eating everything in sight.

For a while Sharon and I just hung out and watched people. Five or six kids from our class walked by. The girls were all taller and looked five years older than the boys. It kind of stinks the way that works out. I guess we get to catch up in high school, or something. And they had that group attitude kids get, like they're way cool. I've never really been able to cop an attitude the way some kids can. I just end up feeling stupid. Maybe it's because I'm an artist. At least that's what I tell myself; artists have always been slightly different from the rest, and some of them may even count *their* steps.

The mall was packed, mostly mothers with their little kids. One woman, with a face like a pug's, had her little boy attached to her belt with a leash. When she was looking in a shop, the boy stopped suddenly and she tumbled over him. She stood up and grabbed him roughly. I half expected her to shout, "Heel!"

At least half the people in the mall were talking on cell phones as they strolled around. It was like they wanted other people in the mall to know that someone would talk to them.

Sharon insisted on going into The Gap, which was OK because it has clothes for boys, too. Then she made me go into Weather Vane and The Limited.

"Let's not look in any more shops," I suggested. "It's almost time for Wong's grand opening."

"Where is it, anyway?"

"The food court."

"Well, let's sit down for a minute. My mom bought me these shoes, and they're, like, two sizes too small."

We sat on a bench next to a potted plant.

"It's pathetic, isn't it?" Sharon tugged off her shoes and rubbed her feet.

"Huh?"

"This is supposed to be love."

"What are you talking about?"

"Look around you! Everywhere. Boys with their arms slung over girls like their arms are wet towels and the girls' shoulders are towel racks."

As if on cue, a couple of teenagers walked by. The girl had bleached hair and a pierced nose. She wore a tank top that was about ten sizes too small, cutoffs, and platform shoes. The boy, who had his arm slung around her, also had bleached hair, only his stood up in spikes on his head that looked like porcupine quills. With his free hand he puffed on a cigarette.

"So?" I said.

"So!" Sharon threw the word back at me. "Where's the beauty, the romance? You know, like what happened to Gable and Lombard, or Hepburn and Tracey."

"You'd think there weren't any movies made after the 1930s, to hear *you* talk."

"You mean 1940s! Really, Aaron, you're oblivious." She gestured to another couple. "If this is love, then I fear for the future of the human race. . . ."

Now she was on a roll. I didn't really want to get into a discussion of romance, but I knew she'd have to finish her speech before she was satisfied. In that way, Sharon was a bit like Bertha when Bertha recited her fractured rhymes. At least I knew when Bertha had finished, when she said, "My name is Bertha."

"Love has been reduced to *slumping*," she ranted.

"It's noon." I changed the subject. "Let's go to Wong's."

chapter 13

◉ ◉ ◉   Wong's was jam-packed. It gave me a kind of sick feeling in my stomach to see it. When the restaurant was across the street from us, there had usually been just a couple of customers at any given time.

Above the shop the Wongs had hung balloons and flags from different countries. Mrs. Wong and Tony's sisters moved through the crowd with a tray of samples: teriyaki chicken, egg rolls, ravioli, and water chestnuts wrapped in bacon. Mr. Wong and Tony's uncle manned the counter with a couple of scared-looking teenagers who'd been hired only yesterday. Tony's aunt was at a big table, passing out his mom's famous seashell cookies and coffee. It was a big party. "Hi, Aaron," she shouted happily, handing us each a cookie.

"Where's Tony?" Sharon asked.

"Near the clown."

We walked to the other side of the long counter, where a large fat man in a clown suit stood, still as a statue. He had a bright red-and-blue face, with a painted white grin. But he didn't look happy. He gazed sadly at the crowd, like he was also mourning the plight of love.

Behind him was Tony. He stood next to a big tank of helium, blowing up balloons for the little kids.

We pushed through the crowd. Pug Mom was being dragged toward Tony by her leashed kid. "Wed one! Wed one!" the kid whined.

Tony gave the kid a fake smile and handed him a green balloon. The kid burst into tears.

"Maybe you don't understand English," the mom barked. "He said, 'Red.'"

Tony looked like he was about to tell her off. But then he filled a red balloon with helium and gave it to the boy. The first rule of owning your own business: The customer is always right.

"I hope she trips on that leash," he said after she'd left.

"Your wish has already come true," I joked.

"Wow, this is really something!" Sharon said. She likes to pretend she hates Tony, but Sharon has a soft spot for him, especially since we had our stakeout last February, when she admitted she liked his parents' cooking.

"Is that clown part of your opening?" I asked. The clown was now tilting back and forth like a mechanical bird.

"Yeah, doesn't he suck? He was supposed to be blowing up these balloons, but he kept filling them too much and popping them. He sent at least ten little kids away howling with fear."

Mrs. Wong walked by with a tray of samples; the clown shot out his arm and grabbed a few.

"Why doesn't your mom send him home?" Sharon asked.

"Too busy." Tony shrugged. "Have you guys had lunch? I'm almost out of balloons. We can go to the back, where we keep the good stuff."

"Why don't you guys sell the 'good stuff'?" Sharon asked.

"The g. p. wouldn't know good stuff if it jumped up and bit them in the butt."

"The 'g. p.'?" Sharon asked.

"The general public," I explained. Her dad's a psychiatrist, and I doubt he calls his patients that.

"Yeah, we give the g. p. worms instead of noodles, and barf in the soup," Tony said. "All the while, we're sucking down caviar."

Sharon punched Tony hard. "You really know how to take away my appetite."

I glanced over at the clown again. Something about him got under my skin, like when you know someone but can't remember his name. I tried to imagine him without his makeup. Then someone walked up to him, someone whose long neck and freckled face I recognized right away; it was the Giraffe who'd come into our pet store.

The clown slapped the Giraffe on the back and said in a booming voice, "You gotta love it!"

chapter 14

◉ ◉ ◉   For the next couple of days, I thought about the clown and the Giraffe. One minute I'd been looking at them in the mall; the next, Tony told some joke about dog poop, and by the time I'd finished laughing, they were gone. The clown never even collected his pay, Tony later told me.

I waited until we were out of the mall and on our way home to tell Sharon about them.

"It could be just a coincidence," Sharon said. "A lot of people use that phrase 'You gotta love it.'"

"I'm pretty sure it was the guy from the library."

"*Pretty* sure?"

X   X   X

I considered telling my parents about the clown and the Giraffe, but then I realized that I should have told them about everything from the beginning; I had already messed up, big time. I had talked to a stranger and given out personal information. I hadn't even told them about the pigeon's note.

By the next week, though, I was convinced that I was imagining the whole thing. No one had come after me for Birdman. The homing pigeon hadn't reappeared. It seemed that if either of those guys was interested in the turtle, he could just ask.

Sharon had gone in the opposite direction. She'd decided that the clown was a serial killer, and the Giraffe was a terrorist. Every minute, she was looking behind us to see if we were being followed. When my parents went to their Weight Watchers' meeting, she insisted I go with her family out to dinner so no one would "bump me off." She was enjoying herself.

Cleveland has really changed. While parts of it, like my neighborhood, are still rundown, a lot of it has been "revitalized." There's a nickname for Cleveland in the Midwest: "Mistake on the lake." It started out as a nickname for the old ballpark. Then some people used it to describe all of Cleveland. For a long time the city lived up to that name. Now, though, you can go down to the waterfront on the weekend, and the fancy restaurants and shops are loaded with tourists. There's a rock 'n' roll hall of fame, a great zoo with a rain forest, the new ballpark — Jacobs Field — and some of the worst weather in the country.

The restaurant where I went with the Trouts was in the nicest part of Cleveland. In the freezing air and fog, though, it was pretty empty, and there was a dreamlike feeling, as if the city had just woken up from a long sleep, like in that old musical my mom loves, *Brigadoon*.

The restaurant was fancy, with white tablecloths, candles, and little vases of flowers on the table. The only menu that listed prices was Mr. Trout's.

Sharon's mom was talking up a storm about a recent golf trip she'd taken to Australia. She'd won the tournament, or whatever it was, and she was complaining that all they gave her was a big statue of a kangaroo.

"And inside its pouch," she moaned, "instead of a baby kangaroo, there were golf clubs. Three of them; triplets. Is that ever gauche?"

"That is so gauche," Sharon agreed.

Sharon's dad ordered martinis for the grownups, and special drinks for Sharon and me. The special drinks came in tall glasses with umbrellas and tasted like coconut and pineapple. They'd fit right in with Mom's decorating scheme.

Mr. Trout is the quiet type. Maybe it's because he's a shrink and has to listen to people blab on about themselves all day. When he looks at you, it's like his eyes are two laser beams. Sharon says he analyzes everyone. It's an occupational hazard, she says, to not be able to have relationships with people without seeing them sprawled out on his couch.

"Do they really lie on a couch?" I once asked.

"Oh yes," she said. "He's a classic Freudian."

That sounded pretty scary. Most of what I knew about Freud's theories had to do with sex — weird stuff about boys being in love with their mothers and wanting to kill their fathers.

Mr. Trout narrowed his eyes at me. *Slightly neurotic artist type*, I imagined him thinking. *Counts his steps. Can't relax until he does his chores.*

"Would you mind passing that bread?" he asked.

I looked down. My elbow was resting in the bread-basket. "Huh? Oh, sure."

"So the Aborigines have these lines," Sharon's mom

was saying, "these songlines where their ancestors have left their music."

I started to get interested. Usually Sharon's mom talks about golf and gossips about famous people like Tiger Woods, whom she's met at one party or another. The talk about the songlines made me think of birds. The variations of bird songs are endless. Birds actually sing just to mark their territory.

"Does each tribe have its own songs; or each person?" Sharon asked.

"Good question." Her mom smiled. "Each *tribe*, I think. But individuals go into the outback in search of them."

"There's a huge problem with alcoholism in Aboriginal populations," Mr. Trout said, stabbing the olive in his martini. "Maybe it has something to do with these . . . songs, or the loss of them. When an individual voice is lost, it's tragic. When a whole culture is silenced, it amounts to extinction."

It made me think of Bertha. Her chattering had always seemed like a code to me. When she'd stopped talking as much, she'd gotten much sadder, it seemed.

The waiter came with a little cart. Every plate was covered with a metal igloo.

The women were served first. Mrs. Trout had a giant piece of sushi on her plate. It was piled high with something that looked like confetti and was surrounded by seaweed. Sharon had skewered chicken with peanut sauce and matchsticks of cucumbers and carrots. There wasn't much on either of their plates. It made me feel a little worried. I was starving.

The waiter slid my plate in front of me. It was chockfull. My hamburger was actually a giant piece of steak in filo dough heaped with thin onion rings.

We dug into our food. The lights got dimmer. A woman set up a cello and began to play. Outside, it started to rain.

"I get to see Bertha on Friday," I told Sharon. "Want to come?"

"Can I?" she asked her parents.

Her dad narrowed his eyes. It was like she was asking to go to China. "We'll see," he said. "I think it's Loafer's day off."

"I can just walk home with Aaron."

"We don't know what the weather is going to do."

"I'm sure you can go, Sharon," her mom said. "Maybe I'll drive you."

"You have that awards luncheon, Mom."

"I'll be finished by then, I think."

After a couple of minutes, I was embarrassed to see that I had polished off almost all of my heaping plate, while Sharon and her mom still had most of their food on theirs.

The candlelight, the big meal, and the music made me drowsy. I closed my eyes; the image came to me of Mom's box. The flaps lifted open all by themselves, and out of the box flew canaries.

"Aaron!" Sharon socked me.

"Huh?"

"My dad just asked you if you want dessert, sleepyhead."

"Uh, no thanks."

Mr. Trout gestured for the check. The waiter padded over.

I looked out the window. It was colored glass that made the outside look like an impressionist painting. For a second I thought I was still dreaming, because there, in all that color, were three faces pressed against the window, staring in at us.

They wore full clown makeup, and their painted clown mouths were turned down into enormous white frowns.

chapter 15

◉ ◉ ◉ On Friday Sharon came to school late, then disappeared halfway through the day, before I got a chance to talk to her. She's part of some Junior Scholars project for kids who are really smart and want to compete in different "bowls." There's the Quiz Bowl, the Spelling Bowl, and Math Bowl. To practice, she gets out of study period and PE.

After school I looked for her. We were supposed to walk home and then go to see Bertha. Her mom was going to pick us up after her meeting and drive us. I could hardly wait.

The Captain had said Bertha was better. Would she cheer up, then, and recite nursery rhymes like she used to? Or would she be sad and quiet like the last time?

The crowd of kids thinned. Tony came by and asked me if I wanted a ride, with him and his aunt. I told him I was waiting for Sharon. He rolled his eyes. But *he* was the one who was busy at the mall most of the times I'd wanted to get together.

I knew it was Loafer's day off, so I looked for Sharon's mom's SUV or her dad's BMW, but I didn't see them. I went back into the building.

"Mr. Betts!" Medlicott rubbed his paws together as I walked into the detention room. He reminds me of a hamster. "And what did you do wrong on this cold miserable day?"

"Nothing," I stammered. "I was looking for someone."

"It's a pity." He gestured to the chalkboard full of writing. "Who's going to erase these for me? No one has detention today."

"I guess you can," I said, then realized how obnoxious that sounded. "I mean, I *would* do it, but I have to find Sharon Trout. Have you seen her?"

"I'm allergic to chalk, and Miss Trout claims she is as

well. You should have seen the display of coughing and sneezing she put on."

I backed out of the room. I could hear Medlicott talking to me as if I were still there. I thought of going into the office, but I knew they wouldn't give me an ounce of information, not if they were tied up and dragged behind a horse. A couple of years ago, Tony broke his arm during PE. When I went to see if he was OK, the ladies in the office looked at me with their prim expressions and whispered the magic word: *confidentiality*.

I waited outside a few more minutes. All I could figure was that she went home early. Once, her mom picked her up in the middle of the school day and took her to Brazil. I sure hoped I hadn't messed up somehow, because I really don't like being told off by Sharon. The tone of her voice when she gets mad is like a cat screeching in the middle of the night.

I waited outside half an hour more. I figured my parents wouldn't be worried. They were closing up shop early today to go shopping. My mom wanted to buy some clothes in new sizes. She'd lost ten pounds. My dad had gained three. Then they had some kind of graduation at Weight Watchers, a party to celebrate making it through the first stage of the program.

I started to walk home. I was on the hundred and fiftieth step when I got to Cross Downs. In the last month, on either side of the condominiums, two new buildings had gone up. One was going to be a restaurant, and the other looked like it might be a movie theater, but still there was no progress on the bar. The yellow CAUTION tape was still stretched around the perimeter of the construction area. The plastic, like black garbage bags, covered the openings. I was almost past the bar when I heard a voice, a hoarse whisper: "Psst. Aaron." It came from inside the bar. "Aaron." I couldn't tell if it was a male or a female voice. It reminded me somehow of Bertha's voice last winter when she had a cold and was telling me a long nursery rhyme about the cow jumping over a hunk of cheddar cheese.

I stopped and looked around. I was on step one sixty. At the end of the construction area, the tape had fallen down, and the black plastic had peeled off and was flapping in the wind.

"Psst. Aaron."

And then I did the second really dumb thing I'd done in the last month. I turned around, stepped over the yellow tape, and walked toward that voice.

chapter 16

◎ ◎ ◎   Darkness always screws me up. I still have a nightlight in my bedroom, like I'm a three-year-old. It's not as if I couldn't find my way to the bathroom, or anything. It's just that when I wake up in the middle of the night, I want to see everything in its place.

I had just stepped over the yellow CAUTION tape. The word *caution* stuck in my mind like a weird chant. I tugged back the black plastic and peered in. I heard a *whoosh*ing sound, like the flapping of wings, as something brushed across my face. Then someone grabbed me and pulled me forward. My legs went out from under me, and I felt like I was on a tilt-a-whirl as I was pulled into the darkness. There were two bodies, one on either side of me: a thin one and a fat one. No one needed to tell me who they were: the Giraffe and the Gorilla/clown.

I thought about some crazy things in the few seconds they had hold of me, like whether Mrs. Gaps would have her baby early, and whether it would look pink and cute or shriveled up like a couple of babies I'd seen. I thought about how busy Wong's was, and I thought about Mom's box. And then it got lighter and the two let go of me. "Walk forward, pet-store boy," the Giraffe instructed. "You're too heavy to carry."

The inside of the building had the same half-built appearance as the outside, except that there were partition boards for walls rather than black plastic. A door opened and a guy appeared. He wore lime green pants, a bright pink shirt, and a ski cap. "I heard sumpin'," he said in a thick New York accent. I figured *he* must've written the pigeon's note. It was like he misspelled even when he was speaking. Only when he opened his mouth and I saw his big teeth did I remember where I'd seen him before, trying to eat chow mein with a spoon instead of chopsticks. It was the Beaver.

"Yeah . . ." The Giraffe whacked the Beaver on the head like he was one of the three stooges. "Us."

They led me into a small room. There was a table, a ceiling light, a big burlap bag, and three stools painted in wild designs. And on one of those stools sat Sharon Trout, a bandanna wound tightly across her mouth. What was worse is that I could see the bandanna was filthy. It looked like a mechanic had used it to wipe car parts. I thought of the word *gagged*. I was pretty sure that gag was making her gag.

It's funny, but I wasn't scared. It's not like I'm the brave type, or anything. It's just that it felt unreal, like any minute someone would turn on the lights and there'd be popcorn and soda.

"Are you going to gag me?" I asked.

"You?" the Beaver said. "Nah. I wouldn't have gagged her, but she just kept yakking and yakking. On and on about what her dad was going to do to me. Worse than a nagging wife."

"Much worse," the Giraffe agreed.

"She rubs me the wrong way," the Beaver added.

I looked at the trio. The Giraffe and the Beaver were standing next to each other. It was clear they were on close terms. The Gorilla was standing away from everyone, holding his head. When he saw me watching him, he whispered, "Sorry kid."

"Please take it out of her mouth," I pleaded. "I promise she won't say a word."

The Beaver shrugged. He went over to Sharon and untied the bandanna.

I could tell she was going to lay into him, and I gave her a look. She closed her mouth and tilted her head toward the window. There, on the windowsill, was the pigeon. It was peering at me and cocking its head back and forth as if it, too, wanted to say, "Sorry kid."

I was glad to see the pigeon, as if having at least one animal in the room made everything OK. And I wondered about Sharon's mom. My parents wouldn't find out I was missing for a couple of hours, if not more. Sharon's mom hadn't known when her luncheon would end. Was she at Betts Pets looking for us now? And if she couldn't find us, would she call the police? Or was she still sitting around a long table, exchanging toasts and witty stories?

"Let's get to the reason for this festive gathering," the Giraffe said. There was something about his voice that made me dislike him the most. It was the voice of the scrawny kid who calls out taunts from high up on the monkey bars where no one can reach him, the one who plays dirty tricks on the teacher, then lets someone else take the blame. Every school has a kid like that.

"Where's our turtle?" the Beaver said.

"Where's our turtle?" the Giraffe repeated.

I wondered what to say. Should I tell them that the turtle was dead and flushed down the toilet? What would happen then? Or should I pretend I had it somewhere, so they would leave and look for it?

The Giraffe walked over to the burlap bag. He pulled out some colored balls and started to juggle. He was pretty good at it. "We want our turtle back."

"I don't know where he is," I said.

The Giraffe shot the balls to the Beaver, and the next thing I knew they were juggling together.

"Tell us by the time we finish juggling these balls or —"

"No more juggling," the Gorilla cried out, covering his face. "I can't stand it."

"Kids love juggling," the Beaver said, tossing all the balls again. "But time's almost up."

"I'd give it to you," I said, "but I don't have it anymore."

"Where is it then?" The Beaver dropped his hands. The balls scattered onto the floor.

"It got lost."

"You expect us to believe that?" As the Beaver walked toward me, he slipped on one of the balls and sprawled out in front of me. I had to try really hard not to laugh; he looked so stupid, his big teeth clacking like he was about to bite into a piece of wood.

"Who did that?" He jumped to his feet.

"You did," the Giraffe sneered.

"I know!" the Gorilla said. "Let's offer them a cut. If we offer them a cut, they'll talk. I had that in mind from the first, when I thought of the kid . . ."

The other two thugs looked at him like he had snakes coming out of his head. "Offer them a *cut?*" The Giraffe gasped.

"Brilliant." The Beaver jumped on the bandwagon. "Just like all your ideas."

"My ideas!" the Gorilla cried out. "You said the Feds would be following us like hawks and we had to fence the turtle, and why'd it take you two days to get outta jail, anyway? You were supposed to get the turtle from the pet shop the day I delivered it!"

"How's I to know there'd be a prison riot when I was being released?" the Beaver whined.

"Why didn't you guys just bring it right to the pet shop if you wanted it there?" I asked.

The Giraffe turned to the Gorilla. "You didn't bring it to the shop?"

"I wanted to make sure the *kid* found it. I knew he'd take care of it. Besides, a big fat guy was always sitting at the counter right by the front door," the Gorilla complained.

Fat? He should talk. The Gorilla was as fat as my dad, if not fatter!

"Even in the circus you screwed up anything that had to do with animals."

"It wasn't my fault they put me with the elephants," the Gorilla argued. "Then they gave me that little bitty wooden fence to hold them. *You* two got to handle the birds. I'll bet a couple of those got away, too, only no one noticed."

"I'm stahvin'," the Beaver interrupted the argument. "So's Pidge." The pigeon flew onto his arm.

"We'll get our turtle first, then we can worry about chow," the Giraffe said.

"The kids gotta eat," the Gorilla argued. "It's suppertime."

"The kids don't gotta eat," the Giraffe sneered. "We're torturing them."

"We are?" the Beaver asked. "Then shouldn't we put a light bulb in their faces, and burn them with cigarettes?"

They looked around the room. The only light was the one stuck in the ceiling.

"All right," the Giraffe said. "Light a cigarette."

"I don't have a cigarette." The Beaver pointed to his neck. "I'm on a nicotine patch. Twenty-five days without so much as a puff."

"What about you, TB. You smoke?"

"I quit six years ago," the Gorilla said. "The power of positive thinking. I didn't even need a patch."

"Well, we'll have to find another way to torture them," the Giraffe said.

Sharon's eyes got wide, but she didn't say a word. I thought about our stakeout, when we met the Captain. We were plenty scared then, but it was just a game. As wacky as these guys seemed, this was the real thing.

"I know," the Gorilla said. "Why don't we do mime? Everyone is tortured by mimes."

The Giraffe's stomach let out a terrific growl. The Beaver's, as if in answer, growled back. "I can't think when I'm so hungry," the Beaver cried out.

"Go get pizza," the Gorilla said, "and I'll work on the kids. Then, when you get back, we can eat the pizza in front of them. That'll be torture."

"You idiot!" the Giraffe said.

"Maybe he's got an idea. It'll take ten minutes to get pizza, tops," the Beaver concurred.

"Me and this kid got rapport," the Gorilla said. "Isn't that right, kid? We're buddies."

I nodded enthusiastically. If we got rid of the other two, maybe I could reason with the Gorilla.

"You?" the Beaver asked snidely.

"Yeah, *me*. Who embezzled the money in the first place? Me and Gozzie. And it was only on account of his getting so sick in the Big House that he was willing to make the map —"

"I'm stahvin'," the Beaver whined.

"Okay. Okay," the Giraffe acquiesced. "Just don't forget to torture them. And here's something that will help them talk." He lowered his long neck into the burlap bag. It reminded me of feedbags they put on animals in the zoo. When he came back out, he was holding something black. I couldn't tell if it was real or just another prop he was handing the Gorilla. But it sure looked like a gun.

chapter 17

◎ ◎ ◎ We sat there for about five minutes in silence. I don't know much about guns, but something about it looked weird. The Gorilla was also staring at the gun; it was like he had no idea how it had gotten into his own hand.

I realized why he reminded me of a gorilla. I had seen this documentary about a gorilla population facing extinction. In one shot a gorilla stared down at the body of its mate, who'd been slaughtered by poachers. Then the gorilla looked back toward the camera, its face full of grief. And that was how this gorilla looked.

"So . . ." He finally looked up. "Did you ever figure it out?"

"Huh?"

"Why they called Stroud the Birdman of Alcatraz, when he didn't have birds there?"

"No." I shook my head. "Maybe it just sounded better than the Birdman of Leavenworth."

"You got a point. And something about islands, you know? 'No man is an island,' the saying goes, but it sure can feel like you're an island sometimes." He glanced over at the pigeon. "Birds evolved from reptiles. Did you know that?"

I nodded.

"What's *TB* stand for?" Sharon finally spoke. It was the longest I'd ever seen her quiet.

"Huh?"

"Your name?"

"In the Big House I told the other inmates that it meant 'too *bad*,' like I am *so* bad. But it's actually what my dad called me when I was little. I would ditch school or get in trouble, and then I'd offer him all kinds of excuses and he would say, 'Too bad.' Then he'd thrash me."

"And I suppose you think that excuses your behavior," Sharon said.

Boy, she knew how to say the wrong thing.

"I'll bet you're an A student, Miss Smartypants —
everything comes easy. All *I* remember about school is
getting this drawing of a skeleton, and I was supposed to
label the bones. It was a test, right before Halloween.
My neighbor across the street had a cardboard skeleton
hanging on the door. A big one with little pegs in all
the joints so that when you pulled a string, the skeleton
danced. That's all I could think about when I looked at
the drawing. Even the tibia and fibula, which I knew
because they rhymed — sort of — I couldn't remember.
I flunked the test, and the teacher made me stand in the
corner. That night I went over to my neighbors' and
stole their skeleton. I labeled every part, then ripped it
to shreds. That was my first crime."

TB seemed pretty worked up now, so I tried a change
of subject. "Did you say the three of you worked in a circus?" I asked.

"That's right. There was a program for parolees, where
we got to work for a circus. At first we were clowns. But
then the parents got wind of it and had a fit. They didn't
want criminals near their kiddies. Can you imagine?"

Uh, yeah!

"So they moved us to the animals. But after I let an

elephant escape, the whole program was canceled." TB peered down at his shoes.

I was sorry I'd brought up the circus. "About the turtle . . . ," I said.

"Tell me the truth, kid, because I want nothing more than to see you out of this. The plan was to leave the turtle and for Cero to go into your shop and buy it. Easy as pie. We didn't expect Cero to be delayed, or for you to make off with it."

"Why didn't you just ask for it back if you wanted it so much?" Sharon said. "Aaron would've returned it."

TB looked perplexed, as if the thought had never occurred to him. I could see that he was a person who always made things harder than they really were.

"Sharon," I pleaded. I wanted her to shut up. We'd never get out of there if she kept moralizing. "The turtle died," I admitted, "and my mom flushed him down the toilet."

"It *died?*" The look on his face was so distressed that I thought about changing my story. "You flushed it?"

"I'm telling you the truth. I don't think all that paint was good for him."

"If that turtle is gone, we're all in trouble. Sorry, kid, but that's the truth. All three of us."

"Wait a minute," I said. "That's it!" I couldn't believe I had forgotten.

"That's *what?*"

"Birdman. The turtle. I drew him."

"You *drew* him. So what?"

"You drew him?" Sharon asked.

"Several times."

"So *what?*" TB repeated.

"It's not the actual turtle you want," I explained. "It's the map. Right?"

"So?"

"You don't understand," Sharon said, picking right up on the chance. "Aaron can draw things exactly — *exactly* — as they are. If it's the map on his back you're after, Aaron drew it."

"Where is it? I'll go get it." He jumped up. "No. I can't leave you guys alone. That's what Cero said."

"You wouldn't be able to find it, anyway," I lied. "It's hidden in a place no one would find in a million years. And by the time those guys get back, my parents will be home and they will have called the police."

"Cero's gonna be mad when he finds out you blew the chance to get the map," Sharon taunted.

"You rub me the wrong way," TB told her.

She stuck her tongue out at him.

"Let's go *now*," I urged. "I'll find the map so you can get whatever it is you're after."

"Five million dollars," he said blandly, as if he didn't think it was possible. "My partner hid it after I was caught, then he got caught. Now that he's dying in prison, he finally decided to fess up to me where the money's hid. It was him who painted the map on the turtle."

"If we go now, maybe we'll be back before they are," I coaxed. "All the pizza places are jammed on Friday nights. It will take awhile."

"All right, kid," TB agreed.

"We'd better hurry," I said. For some reason, TB seemed to listen to me. It gave me a slight feeling of control. We all moved toward the door. TB held up the gun. "Remember, kids," he said, "I've got this."

chapter 18

◎ ◎ ◎   I hoped I had the right idea about getting home. So far I wasn't batting a thousand. I'd given information about myself to a stranger, then practically leapt into a deserted building. Now here I was being led at gunpoint down my own street. And even though the gun looked fake, I wasn't going to take a chance.

I thought that on the way we might run into someone and that I could signal somehow, but as usual, the streets around my house were deserted; no wonder we never have any customers.

As we got to Betts Pets, I peered upstairs just to be sure no one was there. My parents would be gone longer than usual because of the Weight Watchers' deal.

One thing was strange. I could see the light on in the storeroom. It was just a sliver, as if the door was slightly ajar. It was not like my dad to leave it on.

"The drawings are upstairs," I told TB. We walked up. I opened the door to our apartment. Thankfully, I didn't hear a sound. "In my room."

"Go get 'em."

"Okay."

"You sit down," he told Sharon. "I don't trust you." She sat on a chair, with her hands folded.

TB sat on the couch, then looked down quickly and stood up. Hidden under the cushion was a flattened box. He pulled it out and opened it. Doughnuts. The smell made my mouth water. "Chocolate," he said. "Wish I weren't diabetic. Gosh, I'm hungry. I'll bet they're back with the pizza by now."

"There's Chinese food in the freezer," I offered stupidly.

"Your room's that way." He pointed.

I thought about the day I'd come home and found the tank overturned and my drawers opened. So they had been in our apartment. I glanced over at Mom's box under the table. It was still taped up.

"Go on," TB said.

The whole way to my room, I was kicking myself. I

should've said the drawings were in the kitchen. The only phone in the house was there.

I found the drawings and brought them out. TB was still peering into the box of doughnuts, looking at them the same way my dad would. I was surprised he hadn't followed me.

"Here they are," I said.

TB unrolled them. "Absolutely amazing. The details. Now come on, we'd better get back."

"We're not going," Sharon said.

I was pretty impressed by the strength with which she said it.

"Don't worry. I'll make sure you get some pizza, too."

All of a sudden there was a noise in the stairway that leads to the pet shop from our kitchen. I could hear voices and footsteps coming from it. I hoped my parents weren't back early.

"What the heck is that?" TB jumped up and pointed the gun at the sound.

The door burst open and Loafer ran in, followed by the Captain, poker cards still in his hand.

Loafer looked at Sharon, then at me. "You're supposed to be at the nursing home." Then his eyes scanned the room and settled on TB, and the gun.

"Haa!" Loafer spun in a circle. "Yaaa!" he shouted. He jumped high in the air. Then he kicked forward and backward.

It was impressive, but never once did he connect with TB or his gun. It reminded me of the story my mom told about the kid in her class, with the butter knife.

"Who are you supposed to be?" TB asked. "Buzz Lightyear?"

"It worked better on television," Loafer admitted.

TB held the gun up higher. He put his eye to it like it was a rifle. "Line up at the door," he ordered. "All of you are coming with me."

"My good man . . ." The Captain gestured to the gun. "Surely if you want to intimidate us, you'll have to do better than that."

TB peered at the gun.

"Shoot me." The Captain opened his arms and smiled.

TB sighed. He aimed the gun at the Captain. Sharon screamed. TB pulled the trigger. A white flag exploded from the muzzle. BANG, it said in big black letters.

"See ya!" TB shouted, then he dashed down the stairs that Loafer and the Captain had come up. I could hear crashing sounds as he ran through the pet store toward the exit. I hoped he hadn't run into the aquariums, or anything.

Then it was quiet, and we knew he was gone.

"How'd you know the gun was fake?" Loafer asked.

"A brief stint in the circus," the Captain replied. "1952."

Sharon took a deep breath. "We'd better call the police."

"We already did," Loafer said, "when we heard a man's voice up here."

Some chocolate frosting had gotten on Mom's new couch. I grabbed the box of doughnuts and carried them to the kitchen, then came back with a wet paper towel to wipe up the chocolate.

"What in the world are you doing?" Sharon asked. "Cleaning the house?"

But I didn't get to answer because within two seconds, there was another loud noise. The Beaver and the Giraffe crashed through the front door, collared by four policemen.

"You know these guys?" one of the policemen shouted. "We found them breaking in downstairs."

"I only wanted to purchase a hamster," the Giraffe whined.

"And I wanted a little parakeet," the Beaver offered.

"Look at this guy," another cop said. "He's the spitting image of a giraffe."

I liked that cop.

"Who called nine-one-one?" said the other.

"*I* took the liberty." The Captain bowed slightly. "Captain Blue. Detective extraordinaire."

Within another couple of minutes Sharon's parents were there. Her mother started scolding her for being out late, then she stopped, stood stock-still, and gaped at the two criminals in handcuffs — the Beaver crying like a baby, the Giraffe craning his head this way and that like he was foraging for leaves in the trees.

But I could hear what the Giraffe mumbled under his breath: the initials that stand for tuberculosis, a disease of the lining of the lungs also once called consumption, the initials of a man whose dad, like the Birdman of Alcatraz's, didn't think much of him.

"My dear," said Mr. Trout to his wife, "we really should keep better tabs on Sharon."

"There is never a dull moment at Betts Pets," the Captain added.

chapter 19

◎ ◎ ◎   For a long time I lay in bed and stared at the ceiling. I knew I was in for heavy punishment, but I didn't care. I was in my own bed in my own room. That's what mattered. I could feel my old rough bedspread against my chin, could see my framed drawings in the moonlight, the silhouettes of my baseball mitt chairs. I could hear my dad snoring in the next room. There were crazy palm trees and hibiscus on the walls of the living room, a new futon couch and rattan tables, and I loved every bit of it.

I peered at the clock. The bat-and-mitt hands pointed to the four and the twelve on the lit face. There was no point in even going to sleep now. I had to get up in two hours.

I tiptoed out to the living room. The kitchen light was on. That surprised me. My breath stopped. There were things beneath the surface of the world. Who could know if the person they passed on the street was a regular guy or a criminal? Who knew what could happen on any given day?

"Aaron, is that you?"

I breathed and went in. My mom was at the table, with her papers spread out in front of her. The smashed doughnuts were on a plate. Her eyes were all puffy and red, and her hand shook as she picked up a doughnut.

"Doughnut?" she offered.

"No, thanks. Hey, what about your diet?"

Mom shrugged. "My diet seemed very small tonight, even if my body isn't. The police just called. They picked up that other man, near the old brewery."

"TB. Mom. I'm really sorry."

"All night at that stupid meeting, I had a bad feeling. It reminded me of the morning my parents left on their vacation. They wanted an early start. And it was foggy. I had this feeling —"

"And they got in a wreck." I finished the story. "I should've told you about all the stuff that was going on."

"Yes, you should have. I'm surprised you didn't. But things are different now. We don't spend much time together. I wish . . ."

"What?"

"I wish we could go back to the way things were, when I wasn't busy all the time, and we all hung out at Betts Pets together."

"Yeah."

"I don't like changes any more than you do. You come by it honestly." She took the doughnut over to the scale. "There, I weighed it!" She raised it to her mouth.

"No. Stop."

"It's just a doughnut."

"This big fat guy — the one they caught — he sat on it."

Mom looked at the doughnut, startled. She threw it in the sink, then dumped the plateful in the trash. We both started laughing. We laughed for what seemed like twenty minutes. I was surprised my dad didn't wake up.

Suddenly she stopped and stared at me. "What if there are more of them, other than those three. What if —"

"There's not."

"How do you know?"

"There was just the guy who drew the map, but he's in prison."

"Let's hope he stays there."

"I feel kind of sorry for the one guy, TB, the one they caught tonight."

"How could you?"

"It's like . . . he didn't have a place in the world. It's hard to explain. And he really didn't want to hurt us."

"For that I'm grateful."

"Mom, I want to open the box."

"What box?"

"The one from your parents."

"Oh."

"I mean . . . if *you* want to. If —"

"No," she interrupted, "it's okay. Let me just make some coffee." She measured out the coffee slowly, as if she were stalling. I wondered if I'd made a mistake, like walking on someone's plants or breaking their favorite toy.

"Bring it in here," she said, and tugged her robe tighter, like she was bracing up for something. She took out a pair of scissors and sliced through the old, thick tape.

"Mom, you're really losing a lot of weight."

"I certainly am." She smiled and opened the cardboard flaps. She pulled out papers, one by one.

"They're drawings!" I was amazed.

Most of them were in charcoal, but some of them were in pen and ink. There were scenes of sidewalk cafés, with beautifully dressed men and women looking bored and sipping wine. There were drawings of bridges and buildings, still lifes, abstract etchings of train tracks curving onto themselves. There was a drawing of the Eiffel Tower. There was one pastel, smeared and aged. It was of people rushing down a busy street, their bodies tilted like they were made of paper and the wind was blowing them.

They were better than anything I've ever done.

"I thought that was what was in there," Mom said, glancing away, then back.

"These are . . ."

"Mine, that's right."

"Wow."

"I loved to draw as much as you do."

"Why didn't you ever tell me?"

Mom smiled. "Well, Aaron, you may not know this, but my father, *your* grandfather, was an artist. Of course, they died when you were little, so you didn't know them well. He wasn't famous or anything big, but he actually made a living as an artist. In addition to painting portraits, he drew advertisements and illustrated medical books. When I showed an aptitude for drawing, he was so excited. My brother was more interested in sports. Remember Uncle Morty? He came here a few years back and took you to a baseball game."

"Loud guy, right?"

"That's right. I was the focus of all my dad's ambitions. There wasn't anything I drew or painted that didn't come under his eagle eye. My whole life seemed like an art lesson. He even sent me to Paris when I was eighteen to spend six months being a 'real' artist."

I thought about Loafer, his Parisian adventures.

"I'd never been so miserable in my life," she said, holding up the picture of the café. "I wanted to come home. I wrote every week, begging . . ."

"I still don't get it."

"My dad put so much pressure on me." She sighed. "I wasn't allowed to go to a dance, or date, or take up any interest other than art. He obsessed about my talents so much that just looking at a canvas or an easel made me nauseous. And when I got back from Paris, I packed up my things, enrolled in college at Case Western, majored in education, and got a job at Betts Pets. From then on, I did what *I* wanted."

"But didn't you draw anymore, or paint?"

"Nope. I never did. The shop was very busy then. Lots of people in the neighborhood came in daily just to chat. Your dad and I got engaged. Needless to say, all of my decisions were heartbreaking to my father. My parents felt that they had wasted their time nurturing an artist, only to end up with a shopkeeper."

"Wow."

"Yeah." Mom peered at a watercolor of a sunset.

"But why didn't you tell me?"

"I never wanted to . . . what's the word . . . *superimpose* my artistic identity onto yours. I wanted you to enjoy your talents."

"Mom. Can we keep these out? I mean, it would be helpful for me to see them, the way the lines are, the —" I stopped. My throat felt tight and all the words that went with the way I felt were lost inside my head.

"The cat's out of the bag now." She smiled and poured herself a cup of coffee. "I guess there's no point trying to put it back in."

chapter 20

◎ ◎ ◎ Bertha's birthday fell on a family day at Memory Home, the permanent-care facility where she lives. It meant that more than two of us would be allowed to visit her and that there'd be refreshments in the reception room. Mom watched the shop and Loafer drove us in the SUV. We decided to stop at the mall and get Bertha a present.

Sharon had been pretty subdued since we were kidnapped. Her parents barely let her out of their sight. Her mom had even canceled a golf tour in South Africa. It took all the coaxing in the world for them to let her come out with us.

"I didn't know my personality rubbed people the wrong way," Sharon had said after the police were gone, while our parents were discussing the situation. It was as if that were the only part of the whole experience that got to her.

"You make an impression," I had said tactfully.

In the car, she was still quiet. She looked out the window. I could hear her counting beneath her breath.

"Counting your steps?" I teased.

She smiled and peeked over at the three men: my dad, the Captain, and Loafer. They were deep in a conversation about using trash to make birdcages and how they could turn it into a mail-order business.

"My breaths," she said softly. "My mom said that ancient people believed that you had so many breaths in your life, and when you used them up, you were done."

"So how many do you have left?"

"I didn't think we had many left last week."

"*You* wanted an adventure."

"I didn't want to be *that* adventurous. Isn't it stupid those men went to all that trouble for nothing? And now they're in jail again."

"Yeah."

"And that map was from the streets where Jacobs Field is."

"Yeah. Imagine. Five million dollars buried under the baseball stadium."

"I'll bet it's not even there."

"Yeah."

"People will drive themselves crazy over such strange and fake ideas," Sharon said. "That's what my dad says, anyway."

It sort of made sense, even if I didn't understand completely. Things happened in the world every day that didn't seem to have any real reason, just an idea in someone's head that had run itself wild. No wonder her dad was so busy in his shrink business.

"I'll tell you something else," Sharon added. "I'm never going near a circus again!"

Loafer pulled up to the mall. We ran into the Hallmark store and my dad sprung for hats and confetti and a little statue of a basset hound to put in Bertha's room.

We were just on the way out when I heard Tony's voice. "Hey! Spring me."

Sharon gave him a dirty look. She clearly thought that jail jokes were in bad taste. The whole school had been going on and on about our experience. We were kind of like celebrities.

"Sorry." Tony had understood the look. "What I mean

is, where are you going? Can I come? Get me out of this mall and away from these pee-colored artificial lights."

"I guess there's room," Sharon admitted.

"Man," Tony said to me as he got into the car, "I'm gonna have to hang out more at your place."

Sharon gave him another dirty look. When he's around, she feels left out. But by the time we pulled up to Memory Home, Tony and Sharon were competing with gross jokes. And my dad, Loafer, and the Captain had deemed themselves business partners and were planning how to spend their millions.

Loafer got out and opened the doors like an old-fashioned chauffeur.

"My man, you must come in," the Captain said. "There'll be refreshments."

"Yeah," Dad urged. "I've even brought our cards."

"Okay." Loafer smiled from behind his long mustache.

X X X

Memory Home is always heated to about a hundred degrees. Dad says it's because old people get cold easily. The place smells like prunes and musty furniture, but Sharon was polite enough not to hold her nose, even though I could tell she wanted to.

Bertha was in the main room with all the other "guests." She was sitting by herself on a couch near the window, watching a bird hop along a cement wall. It made me think of the Birdman again, how much that first sparrow must have meant to him in his jail cell.

The Captain spoke gently to her about the weather. He introduced Loafer and Tony and reminded her of the rest of our names. She nodded her head as if she understood, but didn't recite a nursery rhyme or call me Captain like she used to.

We ate cookies and drank sweet red punch and watched overly cheerful relatives talk loudly to the other patients in their wheelchairs. Loafer and my dad played a hand of poker.

I don't know if it was the heat, or the lack of oxygen in the room, or our recent adventures, but soon a silence overtook all of us and we stared at one another.

"I know," the Captain said to Loafer. "Why don't you read us one of your poems? My wife has always loved poetry more than anything else."

"Yeah, why don't you?" Sharon urged Loafer.

"I couldn't," Loafer said, pulling a crumbled piece of paper out of his pocket.

"Poetry is meant to be heard," the Captain insisted. "Why, it was originally an oral art."

"The oldest form of literature," Dad added.

Loafer unfolded the paper and peered at it. "Well, all right. I'll read you this one. For you, Bertha," he said, "on your birthday here at Memory Home."

She cocked her head.

"It's my best poem, I think. I sent it to *The New Yorker* last week. 'Bodily Fluids,'" he announced, "by Larry Ospensky."

So Loafer had a name.

He cleared his throat. The paper in his hand shook:

Love be a piece of gum stuck to my shoe
It won't come off no matter how hard I kick
Love be a tongue sticking out of a face
Telling the world it will not be disgraced
Love be a dark town with a single light
To shine in the snow on a winter night
Love be a dog puking on the road
Chasing its ragged tail
Going in circles to no avail
Love be bodily fluids

Be saliva dripping on a chin
Be blood like rivers
Under our skin
Where do my fluids end
And yours begin
Love be ear wax blocking out sound
Love be an earthquake shaking the ground
Love be a rock star bashing
His guitar
Watching its body
Explode into shards

I glanced over at Bertha. Her hands were folded neatly in her lap. And even though she didn't say anything, she had a big smile on her face.

"Wow!" Tony cried out. "That's brilliant. I love that bit about ear wax. Isn't it amazing, Aaron?"

"Yeah."

"The best poem I ever heard!" Tony said.

Loafer peered at each of us, like he was memorizing our faces. He seemed kind of teary eyed. Then he smiled a big smile, and Bertha started clapping. All six of us burst into applause.